'My son and I throughly enjoyed. Both of us laughed out loud. A perfect gift for all those 6 & 7 year olds, **a guaranteed hit!**'

Theo, age 6

'Captivating illustrations . . . Children who enjoy **David Walliams** are likely to be enthralled. A wonderful wacky début.'

Children's Books Ireland

'Very **funny.**'

City Kids Magazine

'A truly magical book. We have found a new favourite author in Harry Heape and **cannot wait for his next book.**'

Polly, age 8

'Had me utterly delighted all the way through. It's **wonderfully original** and consistently **laugh-out-loud funny.** Kids will love it.'

Joe Craig (writer of the bestselling Jimmy Coates series)

All children's reviews provided by Toppsta

HARRY HEAPE is an artist, a visionary and a very successful none-of-your-businessman. A shy and quiet man, Harry lives and writes on the edge of a magical forest where he spends any spare time that he has collecting enamel badges and volunteering at his local monkey prison.

REBECCA BAGLEY lives in Bath (the city, not A BATH, although she did have one once) where she draws pictures so she doesn't have to get a real job. When she's not hanging out in the world of children's books, she'll probably be in a headstand, plotting how to best smuggle a husky into her flat without anyone noticing.

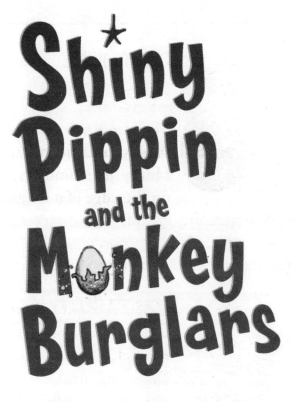

Shiny Pippin and the Monkey Burglars

Harry Heape

Illustrated by
Rebecca Bagley

ff

FABER & FABER

First published in 2018
by Faber and Faber Limited
Bloomsbury House, 74–77 Great Russell Street,
London WC1B 3DA

Typeset in Caslon by M Rules
Printed and bound by
CPI Group (UK) Ltd, Croydon CR0 4YY

A CIP record for this book
is available from the British Library

ISBN 978–0–571–33217–5

1 3 5 7 9 10 8 6 4 2

For Chas and Susy,

with all my love.

HH

x

Twinkle, Twinkle, Little Star

Permit me, lovely readers, to take you back in time. The first thing that I want you to do is to close your eyes and breathe deeply. Okay, great, now open them again very slowly. Are you ready? Good, then let us begin.

One hundred years ago, high in the night sky, a little old star flew through a distant galaxy. It was a brilliant star, the most fantastic in the whole sky, a star bursting with *magical possibilities.*

The star was ten trillion years old and it knew that it was dying. It arced between planets and in and out of comets for a year and a day until it was no bigger than a cauliflower.

It wanted somewhere beautiful to die, somewhere where it could pass on its magic. Finally it spotted our little blue planet and it felt instinctively that this was the perfect place.

It hurtled towards the ground, intent on crashing into a hillside and burying its powers deep within the soil. A farmer saying goodnight to his animals watched it descend above his home.

A travelling circus had made its home on the edge of the town. Very close by, the little star knew it wouldn't make the ground. So it self-destructed and exploded in a shower of very special, shimmering sparkles, which rained down on the hillside, the circus, a mansion on the edge of town, and on the surrounding forest.

The sparkles rained down on the farmer's little cottage, where his young family slept.

They drifted down its chimney and fizzed and flickered and bounced through all the rooms where the farmer's twin baby children slept. In the bed next to the crib the children's mother slept fitfully, having the most fantastic dream. Outside, all was quiet until a little bird began to sing.

Over time, the star's magic soaked deep into the soil, where it waited and it waited. A hundred years later, this twinkly, shiny, brilliant magic had grown into something rather wonderful and this, my lovely readers, is what our stories are all about.

Cock-a-Doodle Yay

Let's start with a lovely big

HELLO!!

It feels so nice to be back, my fantastic friends. You hold in your hands the beginning of the next big banging badventure for

Shiny Pippin and all her magical woodland ~~anipals~~ animals.

Just to send you all a little reminderoony, Pippin is the H to the E to the R to the O – HERO – of our book. She is ten years old (seventy in dog years) and she spends a lot of time hanging out with her twinkly granny. You probably already know that they are two VERY SPECIAL PEOPLE.

They share a massively magical connection, a rather marvellous gift – they can talk to animals because they are Shiny. Don't be silly, a sergeant major's best marching boots and a film star's teeth are shiny, NOT little girls and certainly not old ladies. If anything, old ladies are dusty – no offence to any old ladies having this read to them as their bedtime story.

Well, this is a special sort of Shiny, THAT'S why it has a capital S. It's an ancient, twinkly magic that comes from the stars. It's funderful because it means that Pippin and Granny can talk to Shiny animals and share a special telepathy with them. This magic pair can hear the thoughts of Shiny creatures and the creatures can hear their thoughts too.

Pippin's Shiny soulmate is a little mouse called Tony who she totally Shines with all the time. He spends a lot of time asleep in

Pippin's pocket because it smells of cinder toffee and is always warm and snuggly.

So, to the story. We join them on a beautiful morning. Granny and Pippin were sitting happily on Granny's comfy sofa (so good) eating marshmallows and drinking only the bubbles out of lemonade. They grinned at each other because they were both feeling superb-duperb that they weren't having to battle a scarifying scientist, a pecky-ass penguin, or a crusty, old crocodile, thank you very munch for asking.

Granny's house was in the middle of being decorated and so the little old lady's place was as messy as a teenage pig's

bedroom. Everything was a bit upside down and quite a lot of things were downside up. Granny didn't care, though – she was relaxing and watching her enormous

TeleVision.

Pippin helped herself to another of Granny's deliciously podgy marshmallows. She was enjoying its yummy chubbiness so much that she didn't notice her friend Mungo the geologist arrive with the morning newspaper tucked under his arm.

After her first big adventure, Pippin had decided to use her Shiny powers to do good things and had set up the Woodland Detective Agency. Unfortunutterly, they'd been open for months and had not had a single case. Nothing, not even

 a missing hedgehog, OR

 an owl's stolen spectacles, OR

a mole who'd lost his hole.

To try and generate some work, Pippin had decided to put an advert in the local newspaper. She had spent a very long time coming up with the perfect words for the ad. Mungo had delivered those words himself to the newspaper offices.

'Ooooh,' said Pippin, spotting her big pal at the door, 'is that the newspaper with our advert in it?'

'Erm, kind of yes,' replied Mungo sheepishly. 'It definitely sort of might be ... in a way.'

'Oh dear,' Granny twinkled. 'What have you done THIS time, you enormous cheeky chip shop of a fellow?'

'I can't tell you,' said Mungo

'Oh, come on!' smiled Pippin. 'It can't be that bad.'

Mungo looked sheepish. By this I mean

12

Mungo looked embarrassed, NOT that he looked like a sheep. 'It's a little bit bad,' he said, not making eye contact with either of them.

The truth was, you lovely gaggle of book snorters, that it was of very little consequence WHAT poor Mungo had done with the lovely advert shmadvert. It was ~~irrevelent.~~ It was ~~illeverent.~~ Gaaah! IT DIDN'T MATTER!

Nobody knew it yet, but in just a few small hours they would all be hundreds of miles away next to the roaring ocean, having the biggest, most banging badventure that you could possibly imagine and

I'M NOT EVEN KIDDING.

You are kidding. No, Imaginary Made-Up Robert, I am not.

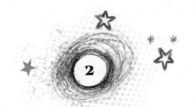

The Good Team

Mungo took the newspaper from under his arm and handed it, very nervously, to Granny to read. The twinkly old lady put on her reading goggles, and began to turn the pages of the paper looking for their advert. She found it eventually, towards the back of the newspaper. I have asked my favourite picture wizard, Rebecca Wiggley, to draw it for us so we can totally understand its vibe. Check it.

In 1972, a crack commando unit was banished to the woods by a military court for a crime against a weasel they didn't commit. They promptly escaped in a wicked-ass fire engine.

Today, still wanted by nine farmers, they survive as muffins of misfortune. If you have a problem, if no one else can help, and if you can find them (Granny's Cottage, Babbins Wood, Funsprings) – then maybe you can hire THE GOOD TEAM.

FOR SALE
SPANISH NAMES!
BUY JUAN,
GET JUAN FREE!!

SECOND HAND
AIR GUITAR
£22.00

FOR SALE
DANCING
KITTENS

Granny and Pippin looked at Mungo with open mouths. It was the little girl who spoke first. 'What ... happened ... to the other, much better words that I wrote down?'

'I'm really sorry!' explained Mungo. 'I was excited and a wincey bit late. I ran to the newspaper offices and when I got there, I couldn't find the proper words! I emptied my pockets but they were just full of conkers and geology and fluff, and I couldn't find the special bit of paper. It was really late and the offices were about to close, so I chose some new words very quickly and that was all that came out of my wonky word-hole. I'm really, really sorry'.

Pippin and Granny looked at each other and smiled because it was rather funny.

'Anyone can make a mistake,' Granny said with a twinkle. 'I think you did a good job under the circumferencestances, and at least you remembered the address.'

Mungo, feeling much better, picked up the newspaper. 'But also, LOOK!' he said. 'I saw this, next to our ad.' The big man was bouncing up and down excitedly. 'This is super-amazing. Maybe THIS could be our first case!' and he began to read aloud.

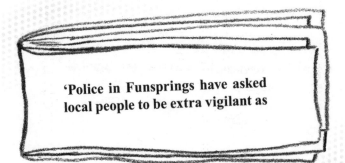

'Police in Funsprings have asked local people to be extra vigilant as

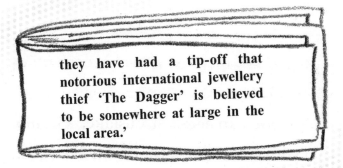

they have had a tip-off that notorious international jewellery thief 'The Dagger' is believed to be somewhere at large in the local area.'

Pippin gasped and looked at Mungo who continued to read.

'The famous thief, who likes to steal from the rich and give to the poor, has been terrorising the wealthy for years with his cunning robberies and taunting police with his super-slick skills. A reward of seventy thousand golden pine cones will be given to anyone with information leading to his capture'.

WANTED!
THE DAGGER!!
REWARD: **100,000** PINE CONES.

DISCO!
TOWN HALL
8PM-10.30PM
NO DANCING.

Just then there was a loud knock-a-doodle-doo at the door. 'Rusty old robots!' said Granny, twinkling like a golden peach. 'Who in the name of wiggly Saint Samantha could that be? I'll just go and see.'

Granny was old and as slow as an assembly – it always took her an hour and a quarter to answer the door. 'Don't worry, I'll get it. You stay and finish your marshmallow,' said Mungo, delighted that he was not in trouble. What the big man didn't know was that once he opened the door, his life would never, ever, ever be the same again.

Lady Elliot

Mungo skipped along the hall towards the front door like a six-foot toddler. As he went he sang a little song to himself because he felt one hundred and ten per cent happy and one hundred and twenty-seven per cent nice. It was a funny song about pretending to be the Mayor of Funsprings, which was one of his main ambitions.

Anyone reading this story, especially grown-ups, must *actually* sing, or put twenty pence in your piggy bank. That is one of the rules of this book and you must obey because I am the captain and somewhere I have a captain's hat to prove it. Sing:

♫ *I'm Mungo,*
Mungo the Mayor.
Everyone knows my name.
I'm Mungo,
Mungo the Mayor.
Everyone knows my name

And all of my games. ♫

The friendly geologist reached the door and opened it. What he saw hit him like a steam train, so much so that he let out an enormous, 'Chooooo-Chooooooo,' for outside, standing on the doorstep, was the most beautiful lady that he'd ever seen with EITHER of his eyeballs.

The visitor spoke in a voice that was smoother than a mole in a velvet dressing gown. 'Good morning. My name is Lady Rosemary Elliot.' She seemed a little distressed. 'I am here to speak with ...

somebody . . . from The Good Team? I saw your ad – I'm very much at my wits' end. I need your help.'

Unfortunately Mungo heard none of her words as he was now officially head

over heels in L.O.V.E. – love. As he gazed besottedly at her, he felt as though he was in the most delightful dream.

If he'd been in a cartoon his eyes would have popped out on two springs, he would have begun to float and red love hearts would have danced around in mid-air above his big love-struck noggin. He looked at the lady and tried to deliver a cool line that would win her heart in an instant. 'I like your hat. Is it real ...? It looks like it might ... be quite ... a valuable hat ... You should be careful in case it gets ... eaten by a ... naughty woodland ... goat ... or something ...' he tailed off.

Oh dearie measles. Poor Mungo. He'd lost control of all of his words. So far, my lovely friends, I think we can safely say that for Mungo, today was not going terrifically well.

Luckily Pippin arrived to help him out. 'Hi,' she said. 'I see you've met my friend Mungo! Do come in. How can I help you?'

'Hello, dear. Are there any grown-ups here? I have come to speak to someone from The Good Team. I saw the ad in the paper and I have to discuss an emergency of the utmost urgency – SOMEONE has INTRUDED into my home'.

'Oh hello, dear,' smiled Granny, joining them. 'My name is Granny but everyone just calls me Granny. We are The Good Team. You've met Mungo. This is my granddaughter Pippin.' She put her arm around the little girl's shoulders and asked the lady, 'So, how can we help you?'

Lady Elliot, it seemed, was not one to mince her words. 'Am I in the right place? You're The Good Team?'

Granny's reply was firm. 'Yes, that's us, dear. We may not look much but do not underestimate us, we are the best in the business. If you want to employ us, please do so, but if you don't, politely say no thank you and be on your way.'

Lady Elliot paused and looked slowly around the room. 'Okay, yes. Quite right. I'm sorry. I'll get right to the point. The thing is, someone has broken into my home and I feel most unsettled. Our family has lived there for hundreds of years but it is a big old house for two. My son George and I often feel as though we would like it a little more full of people, and of life. Being there can be lonely. The idea that someone has been inside snooping about is just beastly. Please say you'll help?'

Granny was a-thinkling and a-twinkling and a-wrinkling her little nose, and Pippin beamed a big smile because she

could see that her granny's marvellous mind was clearly wrestling with something. 'If you don't mind me asking,' the old lady said finally, 'why don't you just go to the police?'

Lady Elliot replied abruptly, 'Ha! Have you met the Chief of Police? He's an idiot. He couldn't find his bottom in the dark with both hands, if you pardon the expression. If he fell into a barrel of sweeties, he'd still come out sucking his thumb. I want to know who broke into my home. I need to feel safe again and, frankly, I don't think the police are up to it.'

Granny looked at Lady Elliot and thought deeply. 'Well ... we shall need to come and investigate, if you want us to that is?'

Lady E smiled an uncertain smile. 'I don't have a lot of choice, do I? Let's shake on the deal.' With that, she and Granny shook hands.

'Why don't you stay for a cup of tea?' the old lady asked. 'We shall finish our breakfast and then you can take us to your home.'

'That would make George and I feel much better,' smiled Lady E. 'Thank you.'

As Granny poured the tea, Mungo, who'd regained his confidence, stepped forward. 'I've been thinking about what has happened,' he boomed confidently. 'It is obvious to me that we are dealing with the greatest criminal mastermind of our time – The Dagger. He clearly broke into your home looking for jewellery. Don't worry, we shall track him down within the week or my name's not Mungo the Magnificent.' He beamed at Lady E, who smiled back at him awkwardly.

Journey to
Helligan Hall

I t wasn't long before they were all squished into the Mungomobile, which was Mungo's big fire engine that he'd converted into an ice-cream van. He'd painted it blue and white and it now had a little ice-cream cone instead of a flashing light. It had a picture on the side to show the sorts of ice creams that were for sale. The Mungomobile was happy – it much preferred being a nice-cream van because it was less smoky and shouty, and not as hot and scary as rushing off to big dangerous fires.

Mungo gave them each a FAB ice lolly for the journey, all of them except Lady Elliot. He gave her a Magnum, which made her feel a tiny bit special.

As they drove, Granny Shined to her beloved Shiny friend Oswald, the big white magical stag, to meet them at Lady Elliot's house, Helligan Hall.

Mungo, because he was excited and slightly nervous, and because he couldn't shut up at the best of times, sang a made-up rubbish song to everyone as he drove his enormous ice-cream van through the sunshine.

♫ *'I'd like to be a dancer*
A-dancing on my toes.
I'd like to be a fireman –
I'd squirt you with my hose.
Tony is a little mouse.
He nibbles lots of cheese.
But there is one thing special
That everyone agrees –
Everyone loves nice cream,

35

Yes indeed they do.
Everyone loves nice cream –
I do,
Do you?' ♫

To help Mungo feel less embarrassed in front of the lady that he loves, I need you to join in the singing. EVERYBODY, or it's another twenty pence in your piggy bank. You know the rules.

Sing:

♫ *'I'd like to be a dancer*
A-dancing on my toes.
I'd like to be a fireman –

I'd squirt you with my hose.
Tony is a little mouse.
He nibbles lots of cheese.
But there is one thing special
That everyone agrees –
Everyone loves nice cream,
Yes indeed they do.
Everyone loves nice cream –
I do,
Do you?' ♫

Pippin was feeling wickedy-wickedy-waaah. It always felt fun to be with Granny, and to have an actual real-life proper case to be working on was very exciting.

'It's obvious that this intrusion IS the work of The Dagger,' announced Mungo. 'I am his biggest fan. I have followed his career since his very first robbery and, I can assure you, this has his name all over it.'

'Really?' replied Lady Elliot, raising an eyebrow, slightly teasing poor Mungo. 'I have a large collection of precious stones and none of them were taken. What do you make of that?'

Mungo had done that thing where he opened his mouth and let his tummy rumble out a load of nonsense, without even thinking about it. 'Well, firstly,' replied Mungo, 'The Dagger was obviously LOOKING for jewellery and secondly, he is supposed to be AT LARGE in this very AREA according to the police!'

'Who are nincompoops,' added Lady E with half a smile.

'I love The Dagger,' continued Mungo, oblivious. 'If we caught him I'm afraid we would just have to have a stern word with him and then we would have to let him go. There's no way I could tell the police. It would be as bad as catching Robin Hood and handing him over to the Sheriff of Naughtyham.'

Pippin, who was listening keenly from

the back shouted out, 'Why exactly do you love him so much?'

'Well,' replied Mungo, 'I love it that he steals from the rich and gives to the poor,' he continued, 'because the rich have too much and the poor, well, they don't have enough.'

'Here, here,' said Granny, munching a marshmallow. 'I like the sound of him too.'

'But mostly,' continued Mungo, 'I like that he is SO cool and funny. There was this one time –' Mungo was already grinning – 'when the Chief of Police put a big reward on The Dagger's head. He reacted by breaking into the police chief's house and stealing all his trousers!'

Lady Elliot gave three quarters of a smile at Mungo, who was now on a roll. 'When the police played back the security-camera footage in the morning, all they could see was a masked man wearing the Chief's dressing gown and eating the Chief's cornflakes while the Chief wandered from room to room, wearing only his underpants BECAUSE ALL HIS TROUSERS WERE GONE!!!'

Pippin and Granny guffawed. They always had such fun together and loved listening to Mungo's funusual nonsense. Lady Elliot looked out of the window. 'I do like that,' she said, smiling fully to herself.

41

The Mungomobile rumbled happily through Funsprings. It passed the town square where Mungo liked to park up and sell nice creams. A gang of children saw them and gave chase shouting, 'Ice cream, ice cream, ice cream.' Mungo hurled loads of FABs and Twisters out of the window and rang his bell.

All the children cheered as the team sped out of town in the direction of Helligan Hall.

Mungo put his foot down and they raced through a tunnel of trees. Light and colour danced off the windscreen as they weaved their way along the wooded lanes. A few moments later they turned off the main road, crunched over gravel and arrived

outside the grand yet rather tumbledown and lonely looking Helligan Hall.

To help you imagine the scene, my favourite picture wizard Chewbacca Biggley has made THIS drawing of Helligan Hall using only a cup of tea, a magic pencil and some enchanted pens. Check it.

fweinds ←

As you can see, Oswald the white stag was already there with his son Martin and Chubby the magpie. 'Hello, peach muffins,' said Granny, climbing onto Oswald's great big back and giving him a massive magical snuggle.

'This had better be good,' Oswald grumped grumpily. 'I was having the best dream ever. I dreamed I was having a lovely long snooze on the comfiest piece of moss in the whole world.'

'Snoozing and dreaming and dreaming of snoozing. Sounds right up your street!' beamed Granny with a very special twinkle in her one working eye.

'Right!' said Martin, for this was very much his favourite word. 'Whatever it is we have to do, let's get cracking!' Martin loved to be busy. He liked to be as busy as a bee. In fact, he liked to be as busy as a bee in charge of a hundred other bees, at Bee HQ, on the first Monday of National Bee Week.

Granny explained the case to Oswald and Martin and asked if they would investigate the gardens for clues, while the rest of the gang investigated inside. 'Right!' said Martin again as his father Oswald yawned. 'We will meet back here in half an hour'.

As they walked towards the big house, something caught clever Pippin's eye. She looked up at the house and saw, in one of the windows on the first floor, a pale face gazing down at the team – it belonged to a boy about her age. Unaware that he was being watched, the boy rubbed his eyes. It was difficult to tell from down in the gardens but Pippin thought that the boy looked as though he had been crying.

Our hero felt a Shiny tingle deep inside her bones as she made her way towards the house. Who was this mysterious boy, and why did he look so sad?

The Crime Scene

As Oswald, Martin and Chubby began their ~~investigatoring investigatorising~~ ... looking around the garden for clues, Pippin and the others climbed the few short stone stairs which led up to the enormous mansion.

Lady E pushed against the big heavy front

door of Helligan Hall with her shoulder and it swung open slowly with an ancient creaky sigh, as if the door was saying, 'More people? Really? I'm exhausted. Don't you know how old I am? Seven hundred and four! That's how old. Well I suppose you'd better come in then . . .'

They all entered cautiously through the ancient moaning door and into the dark hall. Now, my lovely friends, if there are any policewomen, policemen, or police dogs reading this as their bedtime story, they will know that there are several important rules which you must obey when entering the scene of a crime. Firstly you must not move **BLINDLY** onto the scene, in case you **DISTURB** any evidence.

Granny was beginning to teach her beloved Pippin all about investigating. The old lady wanted to impart every last ounce of her huge knowledge to her magical granddaughter so that she could be every bit as much a superhero as Granny had been in her youth.

'Crime-scene professionals,' Granny began, 'always pause and study the whole scene from the edges to build up a strong mental image of every single detail. This is exactly the sort of thing that real-life detectives, like Sherlock Holmes and

Velma from *Scooby-Doo*, would do,' she added, smiling at our favourite hero.

Is this what Mungo did? What do you think? Here's a tiny clue:

NO, OF COURSE NOT!

As soon as Mungo was through the front door, he set off into the middle of the room. 'No, Mungo, wait!' shouted Pippin, grabbing the friendly geologist's hand. 'This is a CRIME SCENE,' she said. Granny smiled at the little girl – she was a fast learner.

'Stop where you are and look around,' said Pippin. Mungo paused and they all looked at the enormous sitting room ...

and saw a scene of utter devastation. It looked as though a herd of buffalo had rampaged through there. Tables were turned over, lamps smashed, a grand piano had been upturned, and a bookcase had been pulled over. There was really nothing in the room that hadn't been totally mucked up.

'Stranger than a duck at a dinner party,' said Mungo, scratching the double stubble trouble on his chinny chin chin. Lady Elliot looked at him. She did not quite know what to make of this big man who seemed full of fun and nonsense. Big Mungo was not like anyone she had ever met.

'We will investigate in here,' said Granny

to Pippin. 'Chubby and Mungo, why don't you search for clues upstairs with Lady Elliot.'

Pippin and her much adored Granny walked slowly around the humongous sitting room with Tony fast asleep in our hero's pocket. The little mouse had found a whole Babybel and eaten it all and was now in a very deep and very cheddary snooze. At one end of the room they saw the most enormous white marble fireplace that you can possibly imagine. It was M to the A to the S-S-I to the V to the E to the massive – you could have parked a hippopotamus inside it.

Our investigators wandered and they wondered, up and down the length of the room several times. Pippin had brought a magnifying glass from home and she inspected every corner for signs of who could have possibly done this. She left no stone unturned which was actually quite easy because there weren't any stones in the room, but they didn't find any clues, not even one clue – in fact, they couldn't even find part of a cl—

Until ... 'Aha!' said Pippin suddenly. She had spotted something odd in the enormous fireplace! She and Granny knelt down and looked through her magnifying glass at some very funusual marks in the ash. 'Very funusual marks in the ash,' said Granny, scratching the back of her head. 'Very funusual marks in the ash indeed.'

As Pippin studied the strange marks, she had that feeling you sometimes get when you know someone is watching you. You know that feeling? Like when you are copying someone's work in a tricky science lesson or picking your hooter at a disco, and you just suddenly begin to feel like you are being OBSERVED.

'Hello, is anybody there?' Pippin called. A boy of about her age stepped out of the shadows and walked slowly towards her.

It was the sad-looking boy that Pippin had seen from outside. 'Hello,' she said, standing up and taking a few paces towards him. 'I'm Pippin, and this is Granny. What's your name?'

'George,' said the boy very quietly.

Granny smiled at him. 'We're here because we are investigating the intrusion into Lady Elliot's home, into *your* home. Lady Elliot is your mum, right?' George nodded.

'You can help us if you like,' beamed Pippin with an enormous kind grin of attempty friend make.

'I've been investigating all morning,' whispered the boy. Pippin, surprised, raised an eyebrow as Granny spoke. 'Okay. Good.' She paused and studied the boy. He was small and skinny with blonde hair which was cut very short around the sides and was messy and stuck up on top. He wore shorts and a green jumper that had patches on the elbows. He wasn't wearing

trainers – he had a pair of old sandals on his feet. He looked, Pippin thought, like a child from a long time ago. 'All we've found are these strange markings in the ash,' said Granny.

The boy pulled out a torch from his shorts' pocket. As he crouched down, his eyes seemed to zoom in on the strange patterns in the ash.

'Odd, aren't they?' remarked Pippin, crouching down. The markings, for there seemed to be two sets, came straight out of the fireplace, across the ashy hearth and onto the carpet for a short distance before they faded and disappeared in the chaos of the room. 'As peculiar as a pig in a poncho,' said Granny. 'I wonder what could have made those?'

George looked at the chimney, the carpet and then across at one of the windows on the other side of the room. His mind buffered quickly, clicked into SEARCH mode and made a list of all the possible possibilities, and also some of the impossible possibilities. He looked at Pippin and said, 'They're monkey prints.'

Pippin and Granny looked at each other, surprised.

'A pair of monkeys, actually,' George continued.

Granny's face looked very serious, shaken possibly, and Pippin didn't know why. 'Odd as a sock,' she said after a long pause. 'Why monkeys? Why all this mess and yet, Lady Elliot said, nothing had been taken …?' She tailed off scratching her mop of brown curls.

'Something HAS been taken,' said the boy. 'Well, not something, SOMEONE'.

'Who, George, what do you mean?' Granny asked.

'Gonathan, my chameleon, has missappeared. I put him in his tank last night before bed and he's gone.' The first glisten of an almost tear began to form in the corner of each of the boy's eyes. He looked down. 'You must help me find him.'

Oh dearie meatballs, George's pet had been taken. Pippin knew how much she loved Tony and she remembered how it had felt when he'd been taken at the beginning of their last, very terribubble badventure. Granny saw sadness emptying out of Pippin. 'Of course we will help,' she said to her friend. 'We'll do more than help, we'll get him back,' she said confidently. Pippin tried to put on a brave face for George but on the inside her heart sank to the bottom of her stomach and she had a strong feeling of 'oh no, not again' ...

Slimportant
Funformation

Everyone had agreed to meet
outside after they had all
done their ~~investigatoring~~
~~investigatorising~~ ... looking around for
clues. Pippin thought that she had plenty of
very slimportant funformation to share and

rushed into the garden, positively bursting to tell everybuddy about the mysterious monkey tracks.

This had to be the coolest case EVER, she thought to herself, a break-in at a tumbledown mansion and the strange clue of the dusty monkey tracks. It was fizzactly the sort of thing you might read about in an exciting made-up storybook and it made Pippin feel seven hundred and fifty per cent excited, two hundred and fifty per cent nice, and as happy as a weekend warthog.

The Good Team began to gather under the shade of a majestic oak tree. Mungo and Lady Elliot soon came out of the

house laughing together and talking about their shared love of rocks, with Chubby flying above.

Lady Elliot had shown Mungo her collection of precious stones. The big geologist had been very interested and had told Lady Elliot all he knew about the diamonds, rubies and emeralds.

As soon as everyone had gathered, Pippin explained very excitedly about not being able to find any clues at first. She told them about finding the monkey tracks that seemed to come out of the fire and bounce off in the direction of the window. When she told everyone that George had said the tracks were from a *pair* of monkeys, she saw Granny exchange a knowing glance with Oswald. Our twinkly hero finished by telling everyone that George's chameleon was missing. SO this was now a break-in and a missing persons' case – MAYBE EVEN A KIDNAPPING.

'His name is GONATHAN and he's not maybe been kidnapped, he's DEFINITELY been kidnapped!' George blurted, looking close to tears again.

Granny could see just how desperate he was feeling and looked at him warmly. 'Tell us how you know that Gonathan has been taken,' she said kindly.

George looked at the lovely old lady. 'I dreamed about him being taken and he HAS been taken.'

'Go on,' said Granny softly.

'He's somewhere where there are lots of big buildings and people and penguins ...' George examined the faces of those around and stopped abruptly after he'd said the word 'penguins', thinking that nobody believed him and that he sounded silly.

Pippin's heart skipped a beat. It had been an enormous penguin, evil Count Visbek, who had captured her beloved Tony in the woods. Pippin had a very bad feeling about this.

'Well,' said Granny, 'thank you, Pippin and George, excellent work, that is all very interesting. Oswald stood up and, stretching, said, 'All that Martin and I found out here was a very large footprint in the flower bed below that slightly opened window.'

'That's the same window that the monkeys were headed towards!' said Pippin excitedly. This was Mungo's chance to join in. 'The Dagger MUST have big feet and he must have trained two monkeys to climb onto the roof, sneak down the chim-chimney, boing through the lounge and open the window for him.' Pippin translated for the listening animals. Chubby flew down and hopped around on the ground in front of Mungo. 'You are are making a big mistake. I'm telling you now – this has nothing to do with The Dagger!'

Pippin passed this information to Mungo, as Chubby continued. 'Upstairs there is an Aladdin's cave of jewellery! Whoever the intruder is, he certainly ain't The Dagger because he left behind all the best swag – the kind a thief like me dreams of. Diamonds, rubies, sapphires and a ton of silver and gold.'

Granny stood up suddenly. 'I am afraid to say that I have a bad feeling in my old bones about this,' she said. 'We have lots of important clues and they are beginning to point in a dangerous direction. Here is what we have:

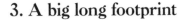

1. Monkey prints

2. No valuables taken

3. A big long footprint

4. And most perplexingly,

A MISSING CHAMELEON.'

Granny asked George to step forward. 'Young man, I believe totally that Gonathan has been taken and that THIS is the most tricky clue so far.' Pippin's eyes flashed towards the boy as her grandmother continued. 'You said that you knew he was gone because of a dream? Tell me all that you know, son.'

George slowly began to tell of being woken in the night by a strange dream about a horrible man and Gonathan telling him about tall buildings and an army of marching penguins.

Pippin stopped hearing the words and the details of George's dream because her mind was swimming in a sea of marvellous thoughts. It was so obvious to her and she was very, very excited. Gonathan had told George about buildings and penguins. TOLD HIM!!! Pippin felt one hundred and ten per cent sure that George and his friend Gonathan the chameleon were Shiners. Pippin looked at her granny who smiled and nodded very subtly back at her.

'Right,' said Granny, 'SOMEONE used monkeys to let themselves into Helligan Hall. SOMEONE with very big feet. SOMEONE who wanted it to look like a burglary but didn't take any valuables. This SOMEONE, for some reason, really just wanted to steal a chameleon. It looks very much to me as though,

THE DOCTOR IS BACK!'

Everybody gasped.

'No!' said Martin the stag. 'I thought we'd seen the last of him'.

'I'm afraid not,' said Granny. 'Oswald and I had one particular run-in with Blowfart many, many years ago, in which he seemed to have trained a pair of monkeys to do his dirty work. They were creatures who he had met on a magical island somewhere.

These monkeys had very strange powers, and were able to sneak in and out of very secure buildings – it was almost as if they could walk through walls. Oswald and I had no idea how they managed it. Blowfart teased us about them – he called them his *ghost monkeys*. I believe that he is working with them again.'

'Ghost Monkeys?' Pippin sounded very interested in these little fellows. Granny rummaged in her bag and pulled out a notebook. From the inside of the notebook, she pulled out several old photos and laid them on the ground for Pippin to look at.

'These are Lumpkin and Bachacha,

HOLIDAY SNAPS - JUNE

Blowfart's ghost monkeys,' said Granny.
'Oswald and I had many run-ins with them
years ago. They are slippery characters and
very dangerous. They specialise in receiving
stolen goods, selling stolen goods, passing

77

counterfeit money and, very worryingly for us, KIDNAP.'

Pippin gaped open-mouthed at this news from the silver-haired crime-stopper with the eyepatch. 'We do not have a moment to lose!' Granny continued firmly. 'Gonathan is in danger. I believe that he is being held at the zoo in the capital city, Great Rock. That fits with the penguins that George has told us about, and has always been a favourite hideout of the Doctor. Mungo, we need you to drive us down to Great Rock RIGHT AWAY!'

Great Rock
(from the Latin
Greaticus Rockus)

Within minutes they'd sped out of the gates of Helligan Hall and were on their way to Great Rock. For Pippin, this adventure was now reading more than one hundred on her adventure meter. As she gazed out of the window and watched the countryside whizz by, she had one big QUESTION swirling around in her head

WHAT ON

EARTH

WAS

BLOWFART

DOING WITH

A CHAMELEON

Pippin turned the question upside down, wrestled with it, tickled its armpits, pinched it quite hard on the bottom, blew a raspberry on its tummy, and shouted, 'YIELD,' but still it did not give in.

Granny had decided to have a little disco nap. Things weren't very easy for her at the moment. The return of Blowfart had opened up many painful memories for the little old lady. She knew she needed to talk to Pippin about Blowfart and the past but there was so much history, so much to tell, it was difficult to find the right moment. Right now though, she knew she needed a snooze to keep up her energy levels – she had the feeling that they might have quite a busy day ahead of them.

Up front, Mungo was at the wheel with Lady Elliot beside him. They were both talking animatedly about their passion for rocks. Mungo loved all of the rocks in the world and Lady Elliot loved valuable rocks that dazzled and twinkled and looked nice.

As he drove, Mungo was happily chatting away like a sausage dog in a sun hat. They passed a road sign, which the grinning geologist spotted and pointed out to the others. The sign looked exactly like this:

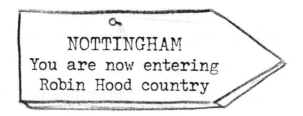

NOTTINGHAM
You are now entering
Robin Hood country

'Gaaah,' said Mungo. 'Robin Hood! My second-favourite thief! I so hope that Chubby is wrong and that The Dagger IS the bad man-guy that broke into your home, Lady Elliot, because I LOVE HIM! You know that he is actually JUST LIKE Robin Hood; he robs from the richards and gives to the poorards – no offence, Lady E,' he added.

'No, I don't mind,' said Lady Elliot, smiling. She was beginning to feel much more relaxed around the big man. 'There is a certain charm and romance about him,' Lady E continued. 'At least he's not just keeping what he steals, like a common thief.'

Pippin, sitting in the back, was listening and smiling at Mungo's nutty nonsense. She thought to herself about how she'd never really been out of Funsprings. She thought about how much her life had changed, about how it wasn't long ago that she had only been able to talk with Tony her mouse but that now she could talk with other Shiny creatures too and was on the way to the capital city, Great Rock, in a massive ICE-CREAM

VAN to rescue a chameleon. *Goodness gracious crikey and plop-a-doodle flipsters,* she thought, *sometimes life can be so ace and funusual.*

As they sped along, she looked across at George who gazed out of the window. He looked anxious and deep in thought. Pippin remembered how she had felt when Blowfart had kidnapped her beloved Tony. She got up and moved to sit next to him. 'You're thinking about Gonathan aren't you?' she asked. George just looked back at her. 'We will get him back, you know. Anything is possible when you have friends that can help you.'

'I don't really have friends,' replied George. 'Apart from Gonathan'.

'Well, I think that you DO now have more than just Gonathan. You have us and we're going to help. I think that you and Gonathan share a really special connection. It's called Shining. It means that you can talk to each other and sometimes you can even read each other's thoughts and communicate telepathically. Granny and I Shine too!'

George beamed. It felt very special to learn that he was Shiny, like his new friends!

THEN, VERY SUDDENLY something strange began happening to George. Pippin recognised the signs and knew immediately that it was a Shine. As it happened, George spoke to Pippin in a trance-like whisper about what was being Shined. This is what he saw . . .

An army of penguins were marching up and down. They were in a big white enclosure with smooth white ramps that curled up to different platforms and criss-crossed over each other above a deep blue pool.

The ramps led to different ledges. The penguins were being led by one much bigger emperor penguin who was huge and strong-looking with narrow eyes, and he drilled his army of smaller penguins, which marched in time behind him.

'Quick march!

Quick march!

Quick march!

Quick march!

About turn . . .

QUICK MARCH!

Quick march!

Quick march!

Quick march!'

The large emperor penguin paused at the top of one of the ramps and a figure appeared at an open window. He was old with grey swept-back hair and a long nose. You know who it was, right? Exactly. It was Blowfart. The Doctor spoke in a vile and feathery whisper to the penguin:

'Excellent work, Visbek. I need you to be extra vigilant today. I believe that we may soon be having some unwanted visitors and NOBODY must enter this place. I am nearly at the end of my work here and shall be moving on to some very important bad business, just as soon as my terrible experiment here has been concluded.'

Blowfart retreated into his lair and stroked a large white fluffy cat who had mean yellow eyes. The Doctor held up a frightened-looking chameleon. 'Look, Gareth,' he said to the cat, 'see how I have entered the mind of the goggle-eyed lizard and I am plundering his powers of camouflage.'

Just like most things in life, Shiny magic has two sides. A good side and a bad side. Good Shining grows out of kindness and light and involves communicating with animals using love and trust. Dark Shining is quite a different thing. It is scary and mean and can be used to take things from animals. Blowfart was using Dark Shining to steal Gonathan's powers of camouflage.

Blowfart showed Gareth the cat his arm. He had managed to turn it exactly the same colour as the table behind it so that it looked invisible.

This process was obviously making little Gonathan very poorly – it was taking all his energy to try and communicate with George. Just before the Shine broke, Gonathan managed to say to George, *I'm feeling weaker and weaker. Please help me ...*

Back in the Mungomobile, Pippin held George's hand to comfort him and looked very intently, right into his eyes. 'So THAT is what Blowfart wants with a chameleon. He wants to learn how to turn himself invisible!' she said.

She also knew from George's description where Gonathan was. Clever Granny had been right – he WAS at the penguin house at Great Rock City Zoo. She'd seen the large white building with its sloping ramps many times on Granny's giant television. She also knew for certain that Visbek, the enormous, terrifying penguin who'd captured Tony during their first badventure, was there.

'Mungo, we must get to Great Rock City Zoo as fast as possible,' she shouted with some urgency. *'No problemo, mon Capitain!'* said Mungo, turning back and grinning.

Hearing about everything in George's Shine made Pippin do a shudder, which she tried her best to hide from the little boy. She looked at George and she hoped dearly that they would be in time to save poor Gonathan who was getting weaker and weaker and weaker and weaker and weaker and weaker and weaker ....

It's Raining,
It's Pouring,
Decorating's Boring

Tony was the only animal to travel
to Great Rock and he was still fast
asleep in Pippin's pocket, dreaming
about winning an enormous banana made
of Cheshire cheese in a card game in a

dearly that they would be in time to save poor Gonathan who was getting weaker and weaker and weaker and weaker and weaker and weaker and weaker ………

It's Raining,
It's Pouring,
Decorating's Boring

Tony was the only animal to travel to Great Rock and he was still fast asleep in Pippin's pocket, dreaming about winning an enormous banana made of Cheshire cheese in a card game in a strange place called Mouse Vegas.

All the other animals had been told they needed to stay behind at Granny's cottage to decorate. That is something that I have tried to write about but it is just way too boring.

In fact, this chapter is so boring I wouldn't bother with it at all. It stinks. You should ask for your money back, maybe even compensation because of how boring it is. It doesn't even have one of Lady Rebecca of Wiggley's magic pictures to snazzy it up.

Here is a list of **three** things which are as boring as this chapter.

1. Traffic jams

2. Rain

3. Rice cakes

Imagine eating a rice cake in a traffic jam in the rain while someone reads this chapter to you – oh dearie meatballs.

Big **Sozzikins** for planting that amount of snoreyness inside your nice noggins. I think it is best for everyone if we just stop this chapter immediately.

Donkeys With
Infections on
Their Bumbums

Meanwhile, you will be glad to know, hundreds of miles away **VERY** exciting stuff was happening. Mungo drove his nice-cream van / fire engine into the centre of the beautiful city

of Great Rock, which perched proudly on an enormous rock on a long conk of land jutting into the wild, wild ocean.

Everyone marvelled at what a beautiful city it was – red-stone houses and shops had been crammed onto every corner of the great rock from which the capital got its name. Rising dramatically at the centre of the city was an enormous red sandstone castle, a medieval fortress full of treasures and surrounded by spectacular ~~Gordons~~ gardens.

Right next to the castle was Great Rock City Zoo and next to the zoo was Timon Keep, an enormous red-and-white striped sandstone and marble lighthouse that for centuries had warned ships away from the dangerous craggy cliffs.

The lighthouse was now in a state of terrible disrepair. Lady Elliot said she'd read that it had been cursed. During a most terrible storm many years ago, the lighthouse keeper had been out of town and nobody had switched on the huge lights at the tower's top, and there had been the most frightful shipwreck. Consumed by guilt on his return, the lighthouse keeper had flown into a rage and smashed up the lighthouse.

The glass at the top was broken and the tower was now almost completely covered in dark green ivy. Local people had tried to repair Timon Keep but had fled, claiming that it was haunted by those who had perished at sea. What had once been a shining beacon at the city's heart, was now a dark and cold needle that seemed to pierce the heavens and suck the light out of the sky. Pippin shivered – she did not like the look of the place at all.

The ice-cream fire engine groaned its way up through the steep streets of the red-stone city towards Timon Keep, the castle and the zoo. Pippin, who'd never visited the city before, was wide-eyed with amazebeak. Bright yellow trams zigzagged up and down the steep streets. Our little hero saw many grand buildings and beautiful statues covered in pigeons, and more people than she had ever seen in her life.

'Well, this is all rather exciting,' smiled Lady Elliot, looking at the bright lights as they whooshed by. And then she began to say something to Mungo. 'I say, why don't you ... erm ... Oh, it doesn't matter ...'

'What?' asked Mungo.

'I was just wondering if you wou— No, never mind,' she tailed off, embarrassed.

'Tell me,' replied Mungo.

'No, I feel too bashful. It doesn't matter.'

'If you tell me, I'll give you ten Twisters,

five FABs and ... SEVENTEEN Soleros!'
Mungo grinned, waving a handful of yummy
ice lollies under her nose.

Lady Elliot returned the big man's
smile, paused, took a deep breath and said
nervously, 'Well, it's two things, really ...
Firstly, I have a little bit of business I'd
like to take care of in town, and I was
wondering if you would care to accompany
me? Secondly, I think you're a lovely
man and I was wondering, if you like ...
maybe the whole evening could be a sort
of date?'

Mungo was so surprised he gave his fire
engine a fright by almost crashing it into

the back of a yellow tram. 'A DATE? Who, me? Are you kidding?' he said blushing so much his head nearly fell off and rolled under his seat. Lady Elliot smiled, and then a huge happy smile-grin of yes boy-oh began to spread across the big man's face. He couldn't believe his ears – SHE was asking HIM on a DATE!!!

Pippin was very excited because it had been obvious all day that Mungo really liked Lady E. She crossed all of her fingers and all of her toes and nudged Granny several times to wake her up and then whispered to her beloved companion about the nice thing that had just happened.

Mungo was a very loyal man and replied, 'Oh thank you, Lady Elliot, I'd absolutely love to, but I'm not sure that I can tonight. I really need to stick with these guys and find George's chameleon.'

'No! You must go!' shouted Granny, twinkling like a golden trombone. 'We can't ALL go and find Blowfart, you know that.

It can only really be one or two of us – you two must act as a back-up.' Mungo listened, looking ever so happy. 'Take this,' Granny continued, dropping a walkie-talkie in his lap. 'Keep in touch,' she said. 'Now. Go. On. Your. Date!' She smiled.

'You sure?' replied Mungo

'Confirmative!' said Granny.

'Are you sure you're sure you're sure you're sure?' grinned the big man.

'Confirmafirmfirmfirmative!' said Granny.

'Lovely!' chimed Lady Elliot. 'Come on, I know just where I shall take you – they do the best poached eggs in the whole of

Great Rock!'

Mungo was so happy that he broke into song as he drove the last little section of the journey.

♫ *'Eggs, eggs*
Everywhere
EGGS
What'll I do?
Eggs, eggs
Everywhere
I think I'll poach nine eggs for you.' ♫

It was a happy song and was directed very much at Lady E. Some of you may be thinking that Mungo, with all his songs, should bring out an album but you'd be VERY WRONG INDEED. I beg of you all, that if you ever meet Mungo in real life, you must promise NOT to encourage him to make an album. If you actually heard the enormous geologist sing you would want to stuff all of Granny's marshmallows into your ears and hide yourself under twenty-six very quilty duvets. The playful buffoon was definitely a nice man but I've heard donkeys with infections on their bumbums that could carry a better tune.

10

Lovely Hooter

ungo was speechless for the last part of the journey. He'd never been so happy and he couldn't smile wide enough. Finally they reached their destination. The big ice-cream van cruised up the side of the castle's Royal Botanical Gardens, next to which was the zoo. They came to a stop just outside the entrance.

Before they farted trumpany – gaah, sorry, I was thinking about something else – I mean before they *parted company*, Granny addressed everybody with a very important piece of information. 'This is a dangerous mission. If ANYBODY GETS SEPARATED then we must all meet at the bottom of the big scary lighthouse. It's the tallest thing for miles around and can be seen from all over the city. It is where we will meet if ANYTHING AT ALL goes wrong. UNDERSTOOD?'

Everyone nodded in agreement. Lady E gave George a cuddle and they all clambered down out of the Mungomobile. Waving goodbye, Mungo turned the ice-cream van / fire engine around and headed back down into town for his special date with Lady Elliot.

Pippin, Granny and the boy George stood outside the zoo. It was now dusk, the sun had gone down, and the zoo was closed for the day. Pippin looked up at the sign.

Great Rock
City Zoo

And as she gazed, she buzzed and fizzed with Shiny energy and very magical

113

feelings. Then something awesome happened – Granny handed out two super-cool jetpacks to Pippin and George, and put one on herself. These jetpacks were awesome. They were like something that might have belonged to James Bond's little sister, Dawn Bond (0015) to help her on her adventures. They were silver with red flashes and they looked as though they had been made in 1952 by Sir Clive Jetpack, the inventor of very fine jetpacks. 'These are very clever, my dears,' said Granny. 'You steer by leaning in the direction that you want to travel, just like a pigeon,' she added with a twinkle.

On the count of three, with Tony in Pippin's pocket still deep in a cheese slumber, they rose gently over the fence and into the deserted zoo. Being inside was super-duper exciting. There was something rather flantastic and funsual about being somewhere amazing that's usually full of people when it is completely empty. The zoo had a calmness that it only really has at night, after all the crowds have gone home for egg, chips, jelly and telly.

Pippin rushed around looking at all the animals. She saw monkeys and zebras and and lions and giraffodils. Haha! Not really giraffodils, that was just me mucking about like a vole on vacation. What she saw was a giraffe standing *next to* some daffodils. Enormo-sozzburgers, my lovely book-ticklers, I do apologise.

Our sparkly hero wished that she could ask one of these cool animals for directions to the penguin house but none of them were Shiny. For an animal to be Shiny, it must have come into contact with the magic stardust that had rained down on Funsprings a hundred years ago.

Suddenly they all heard singing. Pippin turned and looked around but couldn't see where it was coming from. It sounded like an old lady was singing a very funny song while holding her nose. Anyone reading this aloud should hold their nose and pretend to be an old lady to make it sound more accurate and true.

Twenty pence in the piggy bank for any adults not doing the old lady holding her nose voice.

Off you go.

One two ♫
Buckle my shoe;
Three, four, mmm, now let
    me rebember.
Three, four, dog at the door;
Five, six ...
Mmm now what comes after
    five, six?
All the king's poodles
And all the king's men

Couldn't put Humphrey
Together again. ♫

'Hello?' Pippin asked rather gingerly. 'Is anyone there?' Then to her utter good gracious me, an enormous elephant in an enclosure just opposite her looked up and very naturally and in a very friendly old-lady-holding-her-nose-voice said, 'Oh, hello. Very bleased to beet you, I'm sure. My name's Siobhan but everyone just calls me Hooter. I can't rebember why.'

'Wow, you can talk!' said Pippin, dancing around like a banana with new pants on. 'You can talk! How is that possible?'

'Well, I don't really know,' said Hooter, ambling towards the fence. 'I can't rebember.' She was now just a metre away from Pippin. 'Oh yes, that's right. I've always been able to talk. I got the gift fromb by mbother. She was from a circus where all the animals could talk. She did tell me why but you know ... how funny? I just can't rebember.' Pippin was feeling immediately like she LOVED this big friendly and forgetful heffalump.

'We need you to help us,' said Granny, twinkling like a golden guitar. 'We're new in town and we are trying to find our friend's chameleon who is called Gonathan. We

think he might be close to the penguins. Can you tell us where the penguins live?'

'Of course I can,' said lovely Hooter. 'Now lebt me see. If you go up to the top of that hill and turn right. Or is it left? Oh, how funny, I can't rebember.'

'Oh, Hooter, I'm really sorry but this is an emergency of the utmost urgency – we are in a terrible hurry,' Pippin urged.

'Oh, I'm sorry,' replied lovely big Hooter. 'Let me take you there. I'm sure I will remember by walking and not by talking. If only I could get out of here.'

'Why don't you use your incredible elephanty strength and bend those puny

fence posts like they were just coat hangers?'
Granny sparkled, which made Pippin smile
at fizzactly the same time – sometimes it
was almost as though Granny and the little
girl were connected.

'That IS a good idea,' said Hooter. 'Why
have I never thought to bend these puny
fence posts like they were just coat hangers.'

And with that, Hooter wrapped her
enormous trunk around one of the fence
posts of her enclosure and bent it backwards
like it was just a coat hanger, and stepped
out onto the path to join them. She lifted
Granny, Pippin and George up onto her
back and began to trundle up the hill, and

as she walked she sang (twenty pence):

One two ♫
Buckle my shoe;
Three, four, mmm now let
     me rebember.
Three, four, dog at the door;
Five, six ...
Mmm now what comes after
     five, six?
All the king's horses
And all the king's men ...
Hello everybody,
It's Hooter again. ♫

From their lofty position, Granny, Pippin and George had a great view of the zoo. They passed more monkeys and antelopes and bears. They passed a camel and Hooter shouted, 'Hello, Adam!' The camel was very rude and his only reply was a very long and frightfully wet sounding fart. 'Oh dear,' said Hooter, embarrassed. 'I do beg his pardon,' she continued. 'How rude. Some people just give animals a bad name'

Although they did not mention it to each other, Pippin and Granny were both beginning to feel very nervous. Blowfart was potentially just around the corner, holding Gonathan the chameleon captive.

If he *was actually* hiding out in the penguin house, what would they do?

How would they rescue Gonathan?

Did they have a plan?

The day had moved so fast, neither of them had really thought about what they would do when they found the evil doctor. They kept glancing around in the fading light, just in case Blowfart was about to spring at them from the bushes. Soon enough they arrived at the penguin house. What they saw made them both gulp. Rescuing Gonathan, if indeed she was here, was not going to be easy. There was only one way in to the penguin house and it was guarded by a hundred-strong penguin army.

Granny and Pippin looked at each other.
IF they got past the army of penguins,
and it was a big if, they would still have
to face Blowfart and that could mean
a grim fighty-battle against an opponent
who was mean, dangerous and a very
powerful Shiner.

What if he had the ghost monkeys with
him, or a team of alligators, or a cannon that
fired tarantulas? There was just no telling,
my lovely friends, and what's more, they
had no plan at all, not even a rubbish one.

A Nice
Relaxing Poem

I couldn't bear to write the next section right now because it contains evil Count Visbek and he is way too scary, and so I have written a nice relaxing poem instead to help everybody feel nice. It is called 'Beetroot'.

Beetroot

Beetroot
Beetroot
Purple healthy treat root
Come hither to my house with me.

Beetroot
Beetroot
Purple healthy treat root
I long to roast you for my tea.

by Harry Heape

Penguin Peril

Even though it was very lovely, I don't feel the slightest bit better after the Beetroot poem, my favourite book-snuggling friends, and so there is nothing else for it. I really must go on with the story in case we run out of pages before we reach the end.

Back at the zoo, Pippin, Granny and George all crouched and looked at the penguin house. It was amazing: bathed in intense light from a dozen different spotlights, a beautiful curved white space against the now inky star-strewn sky. It looked more like something from the set of a science-fiction film than from a zoo, but this wasn't science fiction, my lovely readers, this was science FACT.

The penguin house was painted the most brilliant white and its clear blue oval pool stretched back towards a large two-storey building where the penguins slept. A pair of smooth white concrete bridges sloped down from the upper quarters over the pool. The bridges crossed over each other in mid-air above the water, with one leading to the penguin house, the other to the side of the pool above a feeding area.

Pippin's heart skipped a beat. She had spotted an enormous emperor penguin, the very large and frightfully frightening Count Visbek. He WAS the penguin that Pippin had met before in the woods around Funsprings during her first meeting with Blowfart. She had feared that it would be him but it was another thing entirely to see him so close by. He was lit from the side by a floodlight and he cast an enormous and formidable beaky shadow on the large white wall of the penguin house.

'He looks even more **massive** than the last time,' said Pippin, wide-eyed.

'Visbek,' said Hooter to the gang. 'It's Dutch for fish beak. He's the most feared animal at the zoo. Even the lions are scared of him. If your friend's chameleon is being held in there, I'd say it would be pretty much imbossible to get himb out.'

Granny squeezed George's hand. 'Don't worry, my love, we've done much harder things,' she fibbed to the boy.

Visbek had disappeared inside the

penguin house or into the shadows. Pippin gazed intently at the mesmerising scene in front of her. The whole enclosure was patrolled by a regimented army of penguins that marched in time to a sneery voice which boomed over and over:

'Quick march

Quick march

Quick march

Quick march
ATTENTION!'

Visbek waddled back out and along the edge of the pool, inspecting his army. He paused in front of a tiny baby penguin who was shaking and clearly very scared.

135

PARP

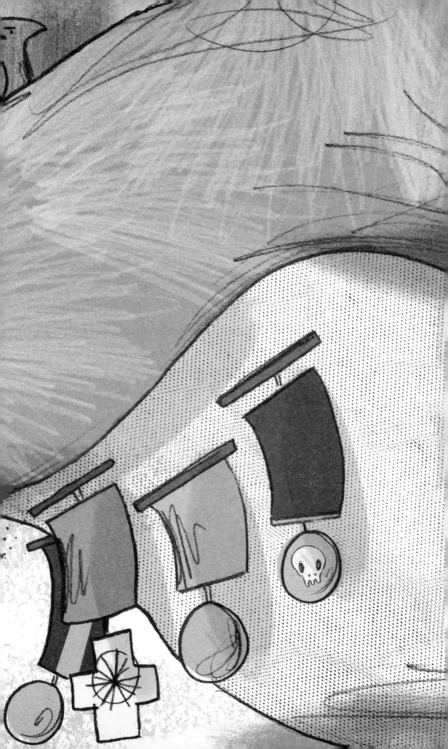

'This is no place for shivering cowards,' he said with a sneery snarl and he kicked the shaky little muffin off the bridge and into the water. Then, without a backwards glance, he continued his drill as if nothing had happened.

'ABOUT TURN.'

The well trained army turned immediately and set off as one on evil Count Visbek's command.

'Quick march

Quick march

Quick march

Quick march.'

Our heroes watched, transfixed. As the

penguins continued marching, they saw Count Visbek waddle up a sloping bridge to one of the windows high up in the penguin house and speak to someone. Just for a moment, Pippin and Granny caught a glimpse of who it was. Although they saw him for only a split second, there was no doubting that it was evil Dr Blowfart. Pippin shivered. She had hoped that she would never see him again, yet here he was, only metres away.

'There's no way we can get in past that army and find Gonathan,' said Pippin quietly. Granny smiled, winked at the little girl and whispered, *'Believe.'* The old lady rummaged in one of her big pockets and pulled out a cat-burglar costume. 'Quick, put this on.' And the Pippin pulled on the trousers, top and hat that were as black as night.

Scanning the penguin enclosure and thinking fast, Granny started to have the beginnings of a brilliant plan. She whispered it all to Pippin, who nodded. They were becoming a formidable team – with Granny's wisdom and our hero's magical energy, it felt as though they could accomplish anything. Pippin just loved learning about adventure and practising her very skillful skills.

Smiling to herself and nodding confidently at Granny and George, she slipped silently into the enclosure and made her way unnoticed around the edge of the pool.

At the top left-hand corner of the enclosure, above the feeding area, was a large metal box – a mechanical feeder that twice a day would let an enormous bucketful of yummy mackerel into the pool for the penguins. This was the clever part of Granny's plan. Brave Pippin made for the box, along the bridge and up towards the mechanical feeder.

Up above, two penguins had spotted Pippin and were waddling off to tell Count Visbek, sure that they would both be given some sort of fishy reward. In a moment the huge emperor penguin was out, sniffing the air. 'Who dares to breach my kingdom!' he boomed into the night, searching the enclosure with his mean little eyes. 'We have a special rule for intruders – they get EATEN,' and with that Visbek began to waddle towards one of the bridges, snapping his big bad beak.

Pippin was safely hidden in the shadows. She had reached the mechanical feeder and had pulled a mini-crossbow, grappling hook and arrow out of her jetpack backpack. She tied one end of the grappling hook to the bucket that delivered the mackerel into the pool. Taking aim very quickly, she fired the hook straight at Visbek. It flew silently through the air, bounced off the wall behind him and wrapped itself around the emperor penguin and tied him in a knot.

'Go, Pippin!' shouted Granny, dancing up and down on the sidelines with George punching the air next to her.

Crafty Pippin then pressed the big red button on the mechanical feeder over and over again. It released a huge bucketful of fish which fell towards the pool and, because it was attached via the grappling hook, it pulled Visbek into the pool and he was showered with a tonne of dead mackerel. The sight of all this food was too much for the army of greedy penguins and they dived in and began the biggest feeding frenzy in penguin history.

As quick as a flash, Granny and George, with their jetpacks on, blasted over to the penguin house. Granny gave Pippin a big well-done high five, followed by a proud and very twinkly smile.

With Visbek and the penguins all taken care of, they went straight into the room where they'd glimpsed Blowfart, to confront him and rescue Gonathan. They burst in, ready to rush at the Doctor but – oh dear – the room was as empty as a shlempty pempty, and evil Doctor Blowfart, who minutes before had been right in this very spot, was now nowhere to be seen.

'Look!' said George rushing over to a table that stood along one side of the room. He picked up a tiny velvet waistcoat. 'This is Gonathan's. My mum made it for him to help him keep warm. He's been here!' He held the little garment to his face, sniffed it, and tried as hard as possible not to cry. Pippin put an arm around the boy and a steely determination coursed through her. The memory of losing her special Shiny friend Tony would always be very vivid inside her.

Our heroes searched quickly for clues as to what the Doctor was up to. In the far corner of the dark room there was a desk, some maps, a computer and a noticeboard. On the desk was a map and a leaflet about the Cleopatra exhibition at the Rocksonian Museum, including a section about an ancient Egyptian artefact, something called The Crocodile Magician's Box, and on the noticeboard there was just one thing: pinned right in the middle, very chillingly, was a photograph of little Pippin, and written above it in large letters were the words:

Granny held a hand to her heart as if she felt pain, as if there was a thorn somewhere inside her. 'My goodness,' she said very sadly to herself. 'What *has* become of you?' Pippin looked on, confused. She did not know what to say and so she did the only thing she could think of – she held her granny's hand and squeezed it very gently.

Chutney

Dearest Readers,

I wish to draw to your attention that this is a really short chapter. If someone is reading one chapter to you before bed then please explain that this chapter doesn't count at all, and you should definitely be allowed another one.

If you are reading this on your own, then you can obviously choose if you want to read more because you are totally in charge, boss of the beach, the head honcho with the biggest poncho, the MAIN billy goat.

As you are chapter captain, you may decide you want to go and get yourself a sandwich and a glass of milk before resuming reading. If you are making a sandwich, I could really go for one too – for your funformation, cheddar cheese and chutney is my favourite. I would appreciate it greatly if you could make it as yummy as possible.

Thanks in advance, from your friend,

Hungry Harry Heape

~~Authorer Writerer~~ Book Tickler & Muffin

Mungo's Date Takes
an Unexpected Turn

In this chapter, Mungo and Lady
Elliot's date takes an unexpected
turn, which is why I have decided
to call the chapter 'Mungo's Date Takes an
Unexpected Turn'.

After they had left the others at the zoo,

Mungo drove into town and parked the enormous Mungomobile a little bit carefully between two very expensive-looking cars. It was really quite hard parking the world's biggest ice-cream van in the middle of a bustling city but Mungo did incredibly well and only bumped the two posh cars a medium amount.

Lady Elliot and Mungo walked arm in arm through the beautiful streets of Great Rock. 'This will be my treat,' said Lady Elliot, with a smile. 'I really hope you like the restaurant.'

'Oh, I'm sure I will love it,' replied Mungo. 'I love any kind of food apart from swede and turnips. I once had swede-and-turnip pie for supper one evening and when I woke up the next morning, my duvet was in a tree.'

'Well, if anyone tries to serve you swedes or turnips, I shall call the police,' said Lady Elliot, smiling. She was beginning to like this enormous silly strawberry mousse of a man.

Mungo continued, 'If this is to be your treat, then I insist that on our next date, the treat will be on me'

'Who says there will be a next time?' replied Lady Elliot. Mungo looked sad for a moment. 'I'm joking!' exclaimed

Lady E. 'The restaurant is just around this corner ... oh?' As they rounded the corner, she stopped. 'I'm ever so sorry,' she said, 'the restaurant used to be there,' and she pointed. What had been a restaurant was now UNDERPANTS R US – a shop selling nothing but thunderpants, and even worse, it was closed.

'Bother,' said Lady Elliot. 'I wasn't that hungry anyway,' she continued.

'Nor me,' replied Mungo, just as his tummy rumbled loudly in disagreement. The truth was that our huge geologist was so hungry he could have eaten ten pairs of underpants. He looked at UNDERPANTS

R US and said, 'Mmm,' quietly to himself and rubbed his tummy.

Suddenly, Lady E pointed across the road. 'Look,' she said, 'the Rocksonian Museum, and the Cleopatra exhibition is on. Let's have a wander round. They have a lovely cafe – we can go there afterwards.'

Mungo looked at the famous museum. It looked amazing, like a huge Roman palace had been plonked in the middle of the city. Mungo counted thirty-six enormous columns around the outside. He grinned because it looked just like the sort of place he would like to run around and be silly in.

'Okay!' said Mungo and they strode

happily, arm in arm through the large black iron gates towards the entrance. To be honest the big man was just happy to be with Lady E – she was lovely and he felt that he would go anywhere with her, even to the dentist.

'Ah look, though,' he said, pointing at a sign by the door. 'It's closing in five minutes. They probably won't let us in.'

'Well, then let's be a little bit naughty and sneak in!' said Lady Elliot. 'It will be fun – come on!' Mungo, as you well know, lovely readers, was not the kind of chap who needed to be asked twice to be a little bit naughty.

Just as the man on the door turned his back for a moment, Lady E grabbed Mungo's hand and before he could say anything, he found himself being dragged into the museum. A second later they were hiding in a dark and shadowy corner under some stairs, behind a huge black statue of an Egyptian pharaoh.

They waited there for what felt like ages, giggling quietly like a pair of giggley gigglers. Finally the last person left the museum and they heard the huge heavy doors being locked behind them. *Clunk*.

'Now for some fun,' said Lady Elliot and she reached into her large shoulder bag and pulled out a pair of roller skates and a plastic pig mask and began to put them on. 'Let's play a fun game called hunt the piggy – it's basically hide-and-seek!'

This date was rapidly turning into the BEST DATE EVER and was like a dream come true for Mungo. Running wild in a museum after closing time was exactly the sort of fun that our friend loved.

'Okay!' he said. 'You better be the piggy first because if I go first you won't find me until Octopril. I am B-A-N-G **BANGING** at stuff like this.'

Lady Elliot sped off on her roller skates. The floor was smooth, polished marble

and she was a terrific skater. She set off
and was soon going about fifty miles an
hour – COMPLETELY SILENTLY. This
museum was probably the best place in the
universe for roller skating. She whizzed in
and out of exhibitions as Mungo counted,
'One, two, three, four . . .'

Lady E flew silently past, statue after statue. She glided at speed into the central area of the museum. This was the kind of place that would make you wide-eyed with wonder. It was as big as a football pitch and would have been open to the sky had it not been covered with a huge futuristic glass dome. Lady E was having fun. She made a couple of circuits of the whole space and was able to get up an enormous amount of supersonic speed before shooting silently into one of the smaller galleries off the central area.

She was having such a blast, weaving in and out of glass cabinets containing

sarcophaguses that looked like THIS

and weird statues
that looked like THIS

and real-life Egyptian mummies
that looked like THIS.

At one point she got up enough speed to jump over the statue of the High Priest of Amun. She landed with grace and continued swiftly weaving in and out of more and more enormous statues. In the distance she heard Mungo – 'Ninety-seven, ninety-eight, ninety-nine, one hundred –' as she glided through a doorway and past a sign which read:

Cleopatra's Jewellery

'COMING READY OR NOT!!!' boomed Mungo's voice from the other end of the museum.

'Oh, I'm ready, my darling,' whispered Lady E. In a flash she changed into a jumpsuit, complete with a utility belt. Next, she pulled out a velvet tookkit. Inside were glass cutters and all the tools that Lady Elliot needed to open up the glass cases and steal the priceless jewellery that had once belonged to Cleopatra, the last pharaoh of Egypt.

Lady Elliot cut the glass in the cabinets and as she did so alarms began to sound all over the museum. Several rooms away, Mungo froze. Lady E emptied all of the cabinets very efficiently as Mungo raced around the museum looking for her so they could get out together.

As soon as Lady Elliot had finished, she skated off silently, planning to find Mungo and hide before sneaking out when the coast was clear. She smiled underneath the pig mask that she was wearing because she was about to pull off one of the biggest robberies in history. All in an evening's work for this cool and clever sausage because, my lovely friends, just in case you hadn't already guessed, in her spare time Lady E was none other than the world-famous international jewellery thief ...

Decorating
(Part Two)

Rice cakes, rice cakes, rice cakes.

Oh
No
You Don't!

Not again. Too boring.

Next chapter please.

Okay (SOZZIPLOPS).

As Strong as
Nine Toilets

Meanwhile, across town back in the penguin house, Pippin stood looking at the picture of herself pinned on Blowfart's noticeboard. She remembered her last encounter with the evil Doctor. He had been searching for a powerful diamond that he called 'El Más Brillante'.

Blowfart thought that this stone was super-powerful and would help him to increase his Shiny powers, but it turned out that El Más Brillante was not a stone. El Más Brillante was in fact a little girl – El Más Brillante was Pippin.

Since then Blowfart had been obsessed with Pippin and was very keen that she join him so that he could use her powers to make himself even stronger.

Pippin was no longer as scared of the Doctor as she had been. She felt that with her granny and her friends and her newly found Shiny magic, she was as brave as a tree and as strong as nine toilets, and she knew that the Doctor had to be stopped.

Pippin looked at George, who was clutching Gonathan's waistcoat tightly in his fist. It made her think of something her granny had said that had stuck in her mind: 'A very long time ago, someone in my family lost their special Shiny friend ... he never recovered.'

Pippin wondered who this family member had been and what exactly had happened to them? She could from time to time see a sadness cross Granny's face, which made her feel unhappy too, and she longed to know everything so that she could try and help.

Pippin's train of thought was interrupted. 'We have to go now,' Granny said, looking very worried. 'We have to go and find Gonathan and bring him back for George.' Picking up and examining the Cleopatra leaflet, the silver-haired lady said, 'It looks like the Doctor has gone to the Rocksonian Museum.'

'Do you know where that is?' Pippin asked her granny.

'Indeed I do,' said Granny, rather matter-of-factly. 'There's no time to lose.' And with that, Granny, Pippin and George stepped outside and blasted into the night sky.

In a moment they were high above Great Rock with the wind rushing through their hair and the ancient city spread out below them. To the east was the wild ocean, with its waves rolling in and crashing into the cold, craggy cliffs.

They hovered in the air for a moment and looked for the Doctor but the dark night sky, save for a few inky-black crows, seemed deserted. George studied the sky urgently. Nothing. They swooped up, they swooped down and they swooped all around, just trying to get a glimpse of Blowfart somewhere in the night sky.

171

Suddenly, George with his searching eyes and fast mind spotted him. He too had a jetpack on and soared high above the city in the distance. As soon as they all had him in their sights, they ZOOOoomed off towards him.

As their jetpacks carried them swiftly through the night sky, Granny pointed at a palace on the outskirts of the city. 'That's where Queen Rastak lives. I've been in there. I did her a favour many years ago – I helped her track down the royal donkey. Queen Rastak thought the old chap had been kidnapped by some bad eggs but Oswald and I managed to track him down.

He'd sneaked into a greengrocer's and was having the time of his life feasting on carrots, bless him. He didn't want to go home.'

Pippin loved how cool Granny was. Even in the middle of a terribubble badventure, she was still full of gleaming loveliness and glittery good times. Pippin vowed to be just like that when she grew up to be a much older grown-up lady lady.

George meanwhile had stayed fantastically focused on Blowfart. The most important thing in the world for him was to find his Gonathan and keep him as safe as a sausage. 'There!' he pointed – ahead of them in the distance, the Doctor changed direction and swooped south. He hovered, clearly trying to get his bearings, and then with a thrust of his jetpack, he was off again, catching an air current and soaring at speed. Granny, George and Pippin followed. They flew over Red Square with its enormous black lion statues and millions of pigeons, who all stopped pooping just for a moment, looked up at our heroes and murmured, 'Coo,' which is pigeon for cool.

Our heroes were gaining on Blowfart. They saw ahead that he had stopped and was circling high up in the air. As they got closer they hung back slightly, so as not to be seen. They saw that he was above a large

Roman-looking building that had a great many many columns and at its centre, a glass-domed roof.

'That, if I am not very much mistaken, is the famous Rocksonian Museum,' said Granny.

'Isn't that Mungo's fire engine parked down that side street?' said the ever-observant George.

They had all expected Blowfart to crash through the roof, but instead the Doctor was behaving with much more caution. He landed gently in one of the trees nearby. What was going on? Why was he not heading inside?

As they approached, they began to see why. The museum was swarming with policemen, policewomen, police dogs and police goats. Haha, not really police goats – don't be silly, they were all dealing with a much more serious incident in a different part of the city.

Our heroes landed quietly, without being noticed, on the futuristic roof of the museum, and slithered carefully on their bellies to the edge of the building to see if they could see what was going on.

It looked like a major 'oh no, dearie me' had occurred in the museum. There were police absolutely everywhere. As our heroes peered down, they saw someone being led out of the museum in handcuffs ... Oh heck-a-doodle-doo, my friends, it was Mungo and he looked as miserable as an elderly elephant walking a poorly goose along a bypass to go to the funeral of a sad old clown. Poor Mungo.

A gaggle of newspaper photographers and camera people had already begun to gather at the gates of the museum where only an hour earlier, Mungo and Lady Elliot had walked happily, arm in arm.

A rather gleeful-looking police chief led Mungo out and headed towards the gathering crowd of onlookers and photographapherphaperphaphers. 'Here's your front-page story, everyone – HE HAS BEEN CAUGHT. The international jewellery thief known AS The Dagger has been apprehended here this evening by the Great Rock Metropolitan Police Squadron.' 'But I'm not The Dagger!' insisted Mungo.

'I sell ice creams! I was just visiting the museum and got locked in by accidon't – I'M INNOCENT.'

'Save that for the judge,' said the smug police chief. 'Sergeant, put him in a van while we clear the area.' With that Mungo, looking very sorry for himself, was roughly bundled into a police van and the door was locked.

Blowfart swooped silently down from the top of the tree to the grounds of the Rocksonian Museum. Our friends watched the evil Doctor in amazement as he pulled Gonathan out of his pocket. He seemed to whisper some strange words and then very slowly, starting at his feet, he turned ALMOST completely invisible. If you looked carefully you could still make out his shape as he walked as bold as brass through an army of police people and in through the main door of the museum without anyone noticing, and a moment later the door was closed and locked shut.

'What are we going to do?' asked Pippin.

Suddenly, the walkie-talkie in Granny's pocket sprang to life and Mungo's crackly voice called out, 'Mungo to the Good Team, I need help. Repeat. Mungo to the Good Team, I need help. Over.'

Granny pulled out the walkie-talkie and

spoke to Mungo. 'Hello, my love. Listen, we know where you are. Hang tight and we'll see what we can do. Over and out.'

Now this was a jam with a pickle on top. How on earth would they rescue their friend? Quick as a flash, with her mind working overtime, Granny said, 'Okay, my dear, I have the beginnings of a plan to rescue Mungo.'

'Good,' replied Pippin, 'because I have no plan at all.'

'You and George must stay up here on the museum roof and wait for me. I shouldn't be long.'

'What are you going to do?' asked Pippin.

Granny grinned from ear to ear. 'Wait and see,' she said. 'You'll have a good view from up here.' She smiled. Pippin wondered what on earth she had up her sleeve. 'It should be quite spectacular,' Granny added with the most enormous twinkle of the day so far. And with that she began to lower herself by zip wire slowly towards the ground.

Mission Improbable

This chapter is one hundred per cent awesome but it would be one hundred and ten per cent much more awesomer if it had a wicked-ass *SOUNDTRACK*.

'Hey, Harry! Let's pretend THAT IT DOES!' ♪

'That's a banger of an idea, Imaginary Made-Up Robert! Thanks!'

So, as suggested by Imaginary Made-Up Robert, I want you to pretend, as you are reading, that there's super-cool music going on in the background. I don't mean gentle flute music that you might hear during a film about an old man who loves fishing, or the theme tune to a show about a stray shaggy sheepdog that has gentle adventures in the countryside. I mean really exciting, edge-of-your-seat stuff – the kind of music that you hear in a film when a man on horseback is galloping alongside a fast-moving train, or a secret agent is making her way out of an exploding building on a zip wire and then lands in a speedboat and whizzes off to a helipad – *THAT kind of thing.*

As the tension increases and the action gets ramped up, I want you to imagine exactly that sort of music inside your brainbox. You don't have to, of course, it's just a suggestion – and I hope I haven't given you indigestion.

Granny faced an impossible mission: Mungo was handcuffed in a locked police van and was being guarded by half of the Metropolitan Police Force of Great Rock. The silver-haired granny-shaped ninja knew that she had to try and rescue

Mungo as quickly as impossible.

Pippin, watching up on the museum roof, was a tiny bit nervmouse. Her granny was actually quite an old lady. She knew she was awesome but she was about to take on a whole police force. 'Be careful,' she whispered in hope.

Down below, she saw Granny crouch and look around her (your music should be starting at this point). ♫

Quickly and silently she sprang like a cross between an Olympic gymnast and a cat, and because she was as light as a feather, she landed with the most gentle of thuds right on top of the police van which held Mungo.

Inside, Mungo looked up at the ceiling. The policeman guarding the doors to the van turned and looked towards the thud, just as Granny slipped silently onto to the windscreen where she clung by her fingers to avoid being seen.

♫ (A little bit more cool music if you please.)

Back on the van's roof once more, Granny pulled a very small crowbar out of her backpack and silently prised up the blue light and pushed it to one side, creating a small face-sized hello-hole.

(Music.) ♫

She popped her head in and whispered, 'Psst!' as quietly as she could

Mungo looked up and a cheeky grin
spread across his friendly face. 'Hello,
Granny,' he said in a whisper. 'Am I glad
to see you.' Unfortunately they had to

maintain total silence, so as not to be caught, and Granny put a finger to her lips, which was the international sign meaning 'keep quiet, you enormous goofball'.

If she had been able to, Granny would have explained her cool plan in an instant and everything would have been much smoother and easier, which together make a new word that I am going to call *smeathier*. However, things would not be smeathier because Granny had to use sign language to try and convey her lovely planny.

Hopefully the big man would understand and would not totally muck up his own rescue like a dog with no pants on. As

Granny looked down at the grinning fool, Mungo mucking up the plan like a dog with no pants on felt like a distinct possibility.

The little old lady put two fingers up to show that she would be back soon, then she pulled up her tights which were beginning to feel a tiny bit bumcomfortable, winked at Mungo, and was gone.

(Music time.) ♫

She jumped silently down onto the ground, did a forward roll and hid at the side of the van, and paused, peeping around the back at the policeman who was guarding the back door.

Quiet as a bidet, she tiptoed towards the

policeman who had his back turned, then lifted the policeman's keys off his belt loop and in an instant had dropped like a ninja to the ground and was safely back behind the van once more. Another silent jump later, she was back on the roof.

Up above, heart beating like a big bass drum, Pippin watched in astonishment and felt her bones tingle with a magic feeling. But this wasn't a Shine, my lovely readers, it was pride and love for her bad-ass granny that our hero was feeling.

Down below, Granny removed a handcuff key from the bunch of keys and dropped

it through the hole for Mungo, giving him a signal to wait for another two minutes. While Mungo was taking off his handcuffs she rifled through her backpack of wicked spy stuff and pulled out a small black sphere.

What was it?

Wait and see, muffins, that's what.

♫ (Music.) Very carefully the silver ninja pulled out a crossbow from her backpack, attached the sphere to an arrow, fired it up in the sky, and counted to ten.

'One, two, three-four-five, once I met a man called Clive. Six, seven, eight, nine, ten, then I met a bear called Ben.'

The moment she got to Ben, high in the

sky there was the most amazing sequence of fireworks that you have ever seen – explosion after beautiful explosion lighting up the night sky and raining amazing fizzing bang-sparkles of glitter-boom down towards the futuristic dome of the Rocksonian Museum.

All the policemen, policewomen and police dogs stopped what they were doing and stood and looked up into the sky, and listened to the deafening bangs and the whooshes and the whistles.

Wasting not a second (music) Granny flipped silently down to the back of the van and unlocked the door with the keys she had taken from the policeman's belt. While everyone was looking at the fireworks (which just kept on explodering), Mungo slipped out of the back door, put Granny on his back and ran around the corner of the museum and hid in the shadows.

Mungo said a very big THANK YOU to Granny.

'My pleasure,' replied the super-skillful old lady.' Mungo opened his mouth to speak but Granny covered it with a hand. 'No time for chatting,' she explained. 'We have important business inside the museum. You wait in the Mungomobile in case WE need rescuing. Things are about to get fun.'

And with that she adjusted her jetpack to nice-and-quiet mode and glided silently up towards Pippin and George, who were applauding the old lady on the roof of the museum.

♫ (Music starts again and then fades out.)

♫

The Crocodile
Magician's Box

he police had all now gone home in their police cars with their police dogs to climb into their police beds and snuggle under their police duvets, where they would dream about receiving medals for excellent battling against bad guys. They had driven away in a big procession, guarding the van which they thought held Mungo, who they thought was The Dagger, but which was in fact emptier than a pauper's pocket.

Inside the Rocksonian Museum, the coast was clear and it was time for Pippin, Granny and George to try and catch Blowfart. They descended in turns on a zip wire through the hole that Granny had made. Once they'd landed inside, Granny flicked the zip wire off the roof. It reeled itself in automagically and she clipped it back on her gadget belt. Watching her cool granny rock the spy game like a bossmuffin

made Pippin feel as happy as a hedgehog
and nine times as proud as a picnic.

Inside, the floor in the museum was marble and was absolutely perfect for ... can you remember what? That's right, roller skootering. Granny, however, would not be roller skootering. She had something else just as good in her backpack and twinkled as she pulled out three banging skateboards. She told them all to adjust their jetpacks and focus the jets *backwards*, so that they could be used as engines for the skateboards.

'Holy Moly,' said Pippin. 'Cooler than an Eskimo's sleepover.'

Having skateboards meant that they were able to travel quickly along the smooth floors of the Rocksonian Museum and in and out of all the different galleries, in search of the evil Doctor.

Our heroes stuck together for safety, and soon were speeding speedily like a bunch of speedsters around the museum. They glided around statues which had once stood more than three thousand miles away on the banks of the River Nile or in the Valley of the Kings in Egypt. They swerved in and out of doorways, past enormous stone coffins and sarcophaguses. Then, from a far-distant corner of the museum, they heard the sharp tinkle-shatter of breaking glass ...

They turned the speed dial on their jetpacks up to eleven and rocketed across the central courtyard of the museum and into a smaller gallery, where they paused. At the top of a corridor, behind an enormous statue of a creature which was half donkey and half kangaroo, they saw just a flickery shimmer of what could have been a person – was it You Know Who?

They put on an extra burst of speed and whizzed towards the mysterious shape. They rounded a corner and all stopped immediately. There, in front of them, was an enormous sign which hung from the ceiling and looked like this:

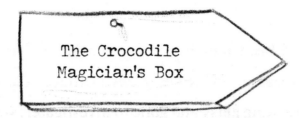

The Crocodile
Magician's Box

Pippin's little heart skipped a beat and her tummy turned an enormous somersault. In the centre of the room was a glass cabinet that had been smashed – inside was an empty velvet shelf. Then came a sickeningly familiar sound which they had last heard in the forest around Funsprings.

Hahahahahahahahahahaha

Just a few feet away, Lady Elliot peeped out from behind a large sarcophagus. She had been hiding, waiting for the police to go home, when she'd heard the tinkle of breaking glass and gone to investigate. Now she hid and watched secretly as Blowfart came out of hiding.

The Doctor was almost completely invisible as he totally blended in with his surroundings, like some kind of weird shimmering alien. He was using his Dark Shining magic to steal Gonathan's powers of camouflage.

'Can you see me?' he laughed.

'Can you see me?'

'Can you see me?'

'Can you see me?'

Hahahahahahahahahahaha

'Give me back my Gonathan,' demanded George.

'I don't think so,' snapped Blowfart in reply. 'He's helping me with my new look. Do you like it?' he continued, laughing. 'I'm slowly equipping myself with things from the animal kingdom that help me in my quest to become the world's most disgusting meanie. Haha.'

'Give us back Gonathan,' Pippin demanded. 'You're finished with him now. You've got what you came for, whatever it is.' She nodded at the small wooden box in Blowfart's hands.

'Ah yes, The Crocodile Magician's Box,' replied the Doctor. 'Legend has it that the box should be opened as close to heaven as possible. I rather think that we need El Más Brillante in a *loftier* setting.'

'Give us the chameleon,' said Granny firmly.

'Not yet,' whispered Blowfart. 'Follow me and I might just hand back the goggle-eyed lizard.' With that Blowfart fired up his jetpack and rose up towards the glass ceiling of the museum and out of the hole he'd come in.

Quick as a flash, our heroes adjusted their jetpacks and set off once more in pursuit. Once they were outside, they paused a moment on the glass roof and scanned the sky. 'There he is!' exclaimed George. Already in the distance, they saw the strange shimmering shadow of Blowfart flying high above the capital and heading back in the direction of the zoo.

Lady Elliot watched them leave through the roof and then ran as fast as she could. She snuck out of a ground-floor window and hailed a taxi. 'To Timon Keep,' she said. She didn't know that Mungo had been arrested and hoped that she'd find him there, as it was where they'd all agreed to meet if anything had gone wrong. 'Hurry,' she urged the taxi driver, who duly obliged and the taxi sped up the steep streets towards the enormous, scary lighthouse.

The Doctor was by now quite far away and our intrepid trio blasted into the inky night sky and flew after him as fast as their jetpacks could carry them. They flew in formation, like fighter planes in a V-shape, with Granny at the front, flanked either side by Pippin and George.

They swooped down through a park. It was SO fun. Pippin loved being a super-agenty, bad-guy-catching, cheeky space-tickler, and as she flew above the swings and the slides, she let out a small hot fart of excitement.

Climbing steeply again over Great Rock Castle, they saw Blowfart circling above the zoo. Rising at the far end of the zoo was the dark and very foreboding Timon Keep. The huge towering lighthouse was so high its top was shrouded in mist.

Blowfart climbed high in the sky, turned and zipped towards the tower, and then landed carefully through the jagged broken glass lighthouse at the very top of Timon Keep. He stood and waited as our heroes circled.

Looking down, Pippin saw Mungo running towards the tower. Ahead of him, she could see Lady Elliot standing at the foot of Timon Keep.

Pippin glanced at her watch but she needn't have bothered – she knew what the time was. It was almost destiny o'clock.

My Lucky Number

Chapter Nineteen. Oh dear. Nineteen is my unlucky number. That IS bad news. My lucky number is 2674. You may not be surprised to hear that my unlucky number pops up much more often than my lucky number. I really wish that this was not so but what can I do?

'You could change your lucky number to seven?'

Well that is a banger of an idea, Imaginary Made-Up Robert! Thank you.

So, as suggested by Imaginary Made-Up Robert, my lucky number is now seven which is obviously much more betterer than 2674.

Here is some more slimportant funformation about me. I like crunchy peanut butter because it is nice and crunchy but I don't like smooth peanut butter because it is way too smooth, and also my three favourite colours are

1. Blue

213

2. Green

3. Bluey-green

What about the story, Harry? Ah. Oh no you don't. You don't want to know about the story. Na na na na na na na. Way too tense and scary. You will have to buy another book.

THE END
(SORRY.)

The Staircase
of Destiny

O kay, okay, it's not the end. Don't buy another book, not until this one has properly finished. I had been trying to avoid this next chapter because it is a section of the book that I do not want to tell you about. I am scarified to know what will happen to Pippin and her friends now that they are about to face their ultimate baddie for the second time – but you are right (as usual, my lovely book ticklers), we do NEED to find out what happens.

Pippin, Granny and George landed at the foot of Timon Keep. Up close it was even worse. It had been a grand building but now, covered with the saddest and darkest ivy, it oozed sadness and despair all the way from its base to its tip, which punctured the clouds and sucked in the night.

Next, our friend Mungo arrived, panting up the steep hill to Timon Keep. He was shocked and surprised to see Lady E. 'What happened to you at the museum?' he said, rushing over. 'One minute you were there, the next, you'd gone? I was so worried!'

Lady E spoke with much urgency to Mungo. 'I will explain later, my love, but right now there's something that you all need to know.' She turned to the others. 'Before you all go up there, that man who's at the top of the lighthouse, I saw him at the museum! He has with him a very dangerous weapon. It's a little wooden box from the banks of the River Nile in ancient Egypt, which contains the most powerful and deadly magic. If he opens the box in front of any enemies, they will be destroyed.

It would be
GAME OVER!'

Everyone froze at this news. Granny looked directly at Lady Elliott. 'The box destroys its owner's *enemies* you say? Are you *sure* about that?'

'Yes!' said Lady E. 'The legend is quite clear. The box destroys the owner's enemies. Cleopatra used the little box to defeat THE WHOLE ROMAN NAVY'.

'I think we should continue,' said Granny with a steely determination.

'Hang on a minute. How do you know so much about this?' said Mungo to Lady Elliott, scratching his head.

'There's lots you don't know about me, my love,' replied Lady E with a wink. 'But be sure about this – if you go up there, you are all in the gravest danger.'

'We MUST go up,' said Pippin, looking at George. 'Gonathan is up there and we have to get him back!'

'Then we will all go together,' said Mungo. 'But you stay down here,' he said turning to Lady E, 'it will be safer.'

'Not a chance. There's no way I am staying down here with you all up there. I'm coming.' And with that, as one, the team made their move.

Granny jumped on Mungo's back and

the big geologist pushed through the large wooden door at the bottom of Timon Keep, closely followed by Lady E, holding George's hand, then came Pippin with Tony still fast asleep in her pocket. As they entered the terrible lighthouse, all the hairs on the back of Pippin's neck stood up. It was as if each hair knew something she didn't, and was trying to make a dash for it.

They bounded up the spiral stone stairs, two at a time, round and around, heading up to the top of the lighthouse. It seemed to take an eternity to reach the top but in reality it was only minutes. Gasping, they turned the last corner and up into the lighthouse room at the very top of Timon Keep. The light had not shone up here for many years, but because it was so clear, the huge moon above the ocean cast a soft light on their surroundings as the team edged around in the half-light before spotting the tall spindly figure of Doctor Blowfart.

'Come closer, El Más Brillante,' he whispered in the moonlight. His words carried softly on the evening air. He was standing right in front of what remained of the enormous light bulb of Timon Keep. He still had the chameleon magic coursing through his veins and you couldn't make

out any of his features, just his shape
shimmering in the dark.

Pippin stood with her granny, shards of smashed glass all around them. The lights and rooftops of the capital twinkled and the sound of the ocean waves rumbled and crashed below them.

'I said come closer, El Más Brillante. I have a proposition for you and I want to be able to see your eyes when I am talking to you.'

'I am only coming closer if you give the chameleon back to my friend.'

'So be it,' said Blowfart and he put Gonathan on a steel beam next to him. The little goggle-eyed disappearing lizard was happy to be out of the Doctor's clutches but he was still very tired after his terrible ordeal and he wobbled very slowly along the beam towards George.

The little boy, breathing hard, darted out of the shadows and lifted his beloved friend to his chest and kissed and cuddled him and told him that everything was going to be okay. Shiny love flowed between them and George could see Gonathan's strength returning before his very eyes.

'Thank you,' George said to Pippin as he reached out and held his new best friend's hand. He wanted her to know that she was not alone in facing the Doctor. Granny spotted this and she too stepped next to Pippin and also held her hand.

Our little hero now felt stronger and more confident as they walked towards Blowfart. Without Gonathan by his side, the Doctor returned to normal and within a few seconds he stood before them – long-nosed, with piercing eyes and his lab coat flapping gently in the breeze.

Edward

Blowfart looked at Pippin and spoke in his vilest whisper. 'Join me, El Más Brillante. I am the most powerful Shiner of my generation, and you are of yours. Together we will be a force that can rule the world.'

'I don't want to rule the world,' said

226

Pippin. 'I can't think of anything worse.' Granny squeezed her hand and the others crowded behind her. 'Refuse,' the Doctor continued, 'and I shall release the power of the box, which will be like unleashing a furnace on a snowflake.'

Granny stepped forward and spoke to Blowfart. 'This is your last chance to do the right thing, Edward.'

'Edward?' said Pippin, turning to face her granny, stunned.

'EDWARD!!?'

Mungo's mouth fell open. 'Edward?'

'Yes, my loves,' Granny replied. 'There is something that I have been meaning to tell you all. I was waiting for the right moment, which never really came. This man, the man you see before you, is my brother Edward. Pippin, he is … your great-uncle.'

Blowfart was cross. 'Edward perished many years ago,' he shouted. 'Edward was weak. He died of a broken heart and became Blowfart.'

'He may have had a broken heart but he certainly wasn't weak,' Granny replied. 'What happened to Edward – what happened to YOU – would have crushed anyone and I don't believe that he is gone. With love, we can bring him back. YOU can bring him back.'

Pippin remembered Granny's words from earlier in the day: '*A very long time ago, someone in my family lost their special Shiny friend ... he never recovered.*'

She had been talking about her brother! Blowfart was her brother and his name was Edward!

'No,' said Blowfart, pacing and wringing his hands together. 'Edward is gone. The only way to end this is for you to destroy me or for me to destroy you. Unfortunately, as we have seen, you are unable to destroy me and so I will have to finish you all off instead.'

'We don't want to destroy you!' shouted

Pippin, stepping towards him. 'None of us have ever wanted to destroy you. All we want is for you to stop doing mean things.'

'We'll all help you, Edward,' said Mungo, stepping towards the spindly Doctor and reaching out a hand. 'Come back with us and whatever made you bad, we can put it right.'

'IT CAN NEVER BE PUT RIGHT! AND MY NAME IS NOT EDWARD!!!'

Boiling with rage, he pulled the box out of his pocket. 'There is only one way for me and it is the ROTTEN WAY. The way of meanness, frightfulness and horridness. It flows through me like lava.

It started because I was a bad person. I am a bad, bad man.'

'What happened was an accident. A terrible, terrible accident,' said Granny. 'When you lost your special Shiny friend IT WAS NOT YOUR FAULT. It was just a piece of the most terrible bad luck. Blaming yourself sent you into an awful spiral, but we love you, and we can pull you out.'

Blowfart paused and looked at them. It had been a very long time since he had felt love from another human being. He seemed to be turning something over in his mind. Granny and Pippin exchanged glances hopefully – *was he about to come back to them*? Finally Blowfart's eyes narrowed and he spoke in his vilest whisper.

'There's only one being who could have saved me and she is gone forever, and it was MY fault. Edward is gone and unless you come with me, El Más Brillante, you shall be gone too.'

'NO!' said Pippin. 'NEVER!'

She made a grab for the box but Blowfart clutched it to his chest and stepping back into the shadows, he opened the box and threw it towards them. It let out the most fantastic bolt of pure energy, which hurtled skywards and bounced off the heavens, returning through the air like an electric sword towards our heroes. Brave Mungo pulled everyone into his enormous frame and tried to shield them in a tremendous protective cuddle.

The magic energy bolt engulfed them like a tidal wave of power, rushing over them and surrounding them in fierce, penetrating light. Pippin and George each squeezed Granny's hands and she drew them closer. Mungo squeezed Lady E tightly. Everybody held their breath ... but the energy from The Crocodile Magician's Box did nothing to harm them – it was quite the opposite. It felt warm and comforting and calm.

The calmness did not last long. The

energy seemed to be pondering something and searching the air around itself, like a huge electric serpent licking its lips. After a few moments, the white-hot electric beast found what it was looking for and turned. In a supersonic rush, it flew at Blowfart, and with a scream of laughter, he exploded into a shower of shimmering sparkles that rained down inside the lighthouse. And as they did so, Blowfart's laugh could be heard getting fainter and fainter until the last sparkle disappeared.

Hahahahahahahaha ....

'No!' cried Granny, and she sank to her knees. Pippin and George knelt down beside her and hugged her. All was silent but for the beating of their hearts. After an eternity, they pulled apart. 'What happened, Gran?' asked Pippin, blinking from the bright light of the energy rush.

'I don't know, my love, but I feel so bad. I feel guilty that I put you in danger. I thought I was going to be able to bring Edward back. I really thought that seeing all his family might be enough to help him change.'

'I'm so sorry, Gran,' said Pippin, looking up at the old lady.

'Why didn't the box's magic work on Pippin?' asked George, blinking.

'I think I know,' replied Granny.

'Something that Lady Elliot said earlier helped me understand. The box would only hurt Edward's enemies,' she continued. 'We are not his enemies, my darling. He is my brother and I love him, and little Pippin does not have a hateful bone in her body, none of us do. The most dangerous opponent of Edward is *Edward himself.* He is literally his own worst enemy. The box knew this and that's why it turned on him.'

Pippin looked through the smashed glass casing of the great light and across the city, lost in thought. 'He'll be back though won't he?' she asked.

'I have no doubt,' replied Granny, picking

up The Crocodile Magician's Box and putting it in her pocket. 'I am not sure how, but he can come back again and again. Our job is to try and bring him back to *us*. That has always been my mission.'

'I want it as my mission too,' replied Pippin. 'I want to bring Uncle Edward back, to good and for good.'

Granny pulled everybody in for a hug and kissed both the children's heads. She reached into her pocket and pulled out a marshmallow for everyone.

THE PRETEND END

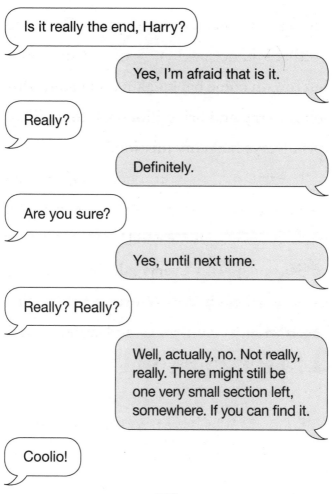

239

Here It Is

Of course it's not really the end, you lovely bunch of peach-flavoured tickle muffins, there are still **THREE THINGS** that you need to know before we're done that will make you feel one hundred and twenty-seven per cent happy and four hundred and nine per cent nice.

The First Thing

After their adventure at the top of Timon Keep, they went back to the zoo and kindly kidnapped Hooter the elephant so that she could come and live in Granny's garden! And sing one two, buckle my shoe, in the sunshine.

Q) How adorable is that?

A) Very adorable indeed.

The Second Thing

On the journey home, Lady Elliot came clean and told Mungo the truth about what

had happened in the Rocksonian Museum –
that she was THE DAGGER. This had the
effect of making Mungo love her a hundred
and twenty million times more than before.
'I am so sorry, my dear,' said Lady E to the
big man. 'I knew that Cleopatra's jewels
were in town and I just couldn't help myself.
I rather fancied stealing them for the fun of
it and then returning them to Egypt. Can
you ever forgive me?'

'Forgive you?' blurted the big man. 'The
fact that you couldn't help yourself just
makes me love you even more than the even
more from before! I can almost NEVER
help myself!'

Pippin and her granny looked at one and other and giggled in agreement.

The Third Thing

The third thing happened just after Lady Elliot had told Mungo the truth. The lovely big geologist pulled over and parked his fire-engine ice-cream van and looked at Lady Elliot and said, 'I love you and I loved The Dagger. Now that I know that you are both the same person, I don't think I will ever love anyone else half as much – WILL YOU MARRY ME?!'

'I'D LOVE TO!' beamed Lady Elliot and everybody cheered, which woke Tony up. He popped his head out of Pippin's pocket and said, 'Mmm, what a lovely cheesey sleep. What did I miss?'

'Oh, nothing much,' said Granny with a twinkle. 'We've just had a day out at the zoo,' which made everyone laugh.

George slipped his hand into his mother's. You could see that the little boy was as pleased as punch to have a cool jewellery thief for a mother. She told him everything and George was now very keen that he and Gonathan should become her apprentices. I think that a disappearing lizard could be quite a useful sidekick for a thief, don't you?

Fumbling in her pocket, Lady Elliot

pulled out a couple of rings. 'Let's borrow these!' she said, turning to Mungo. 'Yours used to belong to King Khufu. He built the Great Pyramid,' she announced, looking as happy as a milkshake. 'We can return them honeymooning on the Nile!'

'Now you're just showing off, you naughty little coconut!' said Mungo, smiling, as they slipped their rings on.

George punched the air and said, 'Yes!' The little lad was delighted at the idea of a big kind ice-cream man / geologist being in his family – mostly because he knew now that he would never go short of Magnums, Twisters or 99s ever again.

THE LOVELY END

Mmmm.
Those last three things *were* nice.

Thank you.

Aw. You're welcome.

Goodbye.

See you soon.

Yes, see you very soon.
HH
XXXXXXXXX